Snow White put down
her broom and sighed.

3

Every day the seven dwarfs left
muddy boots in the kitchen and
dropped their jackets on the floor.

5

They never took off their hats.

They only wanted to be fed.

"What's cooking?"

"I'm starving!"

"Hurry up!"

When they sat at the table, the
dwarfs had terrible manners.

And they never ever cleaned
the table or helped with
the washing up.

9

One day, Snow White lost her temper. "All you want is a housekeeper," she cried. "You don't care about me!"

The dwarfs stared at her
in amazement.

11

"But we adore you," said one.

"You are the loveliest in the land," cried another.

"We'd be lost without you!" said a third.

"Huh," muttered Snow White,
but she went to put a pie in
the oven anyway.

Far away, a wise Queen lived in a castle. She believed that everyone in her kingdom should share the cooking and cleaning.

That way everyone would
be happy.

15

One day, the Queen picked up
her magic mirror.
"Mirror, mirror in my hand, does
someone need me in my land?"

"Snow White needs you," replied the mirror straight away. "The seven dwarfs are treating her like a slave."

The Queen visited Snow White.
"Why do you let the dwarfs
get away with it?" she asked.

"They say they'd be lost without me," replied Snow White.

"We'll see about that." said the Queen. She cut out a piece from a magic apple.

"Pretend you've been poisoned and see what the dwarfs say when they find you."

That evening, the seven
dwarfs marched in the door,
threw off their boots and shouted
for their supper.

Then they saw Snow White
lying on the floor with the
apple beside her.

"Oh, no!" cried the dwarfs. "That apple is poisoned! Snow White is dead!" They all burst into tears.

"Who's going to cook our food?"

"Who's going to clean our house?"

"Who's going to wash our clothes?"

Snow White got up from the floor
and gave the seven dwarfs
a long, hard stare.

"Wash your own dishes!" she said.

"I'm leaving!"

And guess what? Snow White found a nice prince and lived very happily ever after.

Puzzle 1

Put these pictures in the correct order.
Which event do you think is most important?
Now try writing the story in your own words!

Puzzle 2

Choose the correct speech bubbles for each character. Can you think of any others? Turn over to find the answers.

Answers

Puzzle 1

The correct order is: 1f, 2d, 3e, 4a, 5c, 6b

Puzzle 2

Snow White: 2, 3

The seven dwarfs: 5, 6

The Queen: 1, 4

Look out for more Hopscotch Twisty Tales and Fairy Tales:

TWISTY TALES

The Princess and the Frozen Peas
ISBN 978 1 4451 0669 4*
ISBN 978 1 4451 0675 5

Snow White Sees the Light
ISBN 978 1 4451 0670 0*
ISBN 978 1 4451 0676 2

The Elves and the Trendy Shoes
ISBN 978 1 4451 0672 4*
ISBN 978 1 4451 0678 6

The Three Frilly Goats Fluff
ISBN 978 1 4451 0671 7*
ISBN 978 1 4451 0677 9

Princess Frog
ISBN 978 1 4451 0673 1*
ISBN 978 1 4451 0679 3

Rumpled Stilton Skin
ISBN 978 1 4451 0674 8*
ISBN 978 1 4451 0680 9

Jack and the Bean Pie
ISBN 978 1 4451 0182 8

Brownilocks and the Three Bowls of Cornflakes
ISBN 978 1 4451 0183 5

Cinderella's Big Foot
ISBN 978 1 4451 0184 2

Little Bad Riding Hood
ISBN 978 1 4451 0185 9

Sleeping Beauty – 100 Years Later
ISBN 978 1 4451 0186 6

FAIRY TALES

The Three Little Pigs
ISBN 978 0 7496 7905 7

Little Red Riding Hood
ISBN 978 0 7496 7907 1

Goldilocks and the Three Bears
ISBN 978 0 7496 7903 3

Hansel and Gretel
ISBN 978 0 7496 7904 0

Rapunzel
ISBN 978 0 7496 7906 4

Rumpelstiltskin
ISBN 978 0 7496 7908 8

The Elves and the Shoemaker
ISBN 978 0 7496 8543 0

The Ugly Duckling
ISBN 978 0 7496 8544 7

Sleeping Beauty
ISBN 978 0 7496 8545 4

The Frog Prince
ISBN 978 0 7496 8546 1

The Princess and the Pea
ISBN 978 0 7496 8547 8

Dick Whittington
ISBN 978 0 7496 8548 5

Cinderella
ISBN 978 0 7496 7417 5

Snow White and the Seven Dwarfs
ISBN 978 0 7496 7418 2

The Pied Piper of Hamelin
ISBN 978 0 7496 7419 9

Jack and the Beanstalk
ISBN 978 0 7496 7422 9

The Three Billy Goats Gruff
ISBN 978 0 7496 7420 5

For more Hopscotch books go to:
www.franklinwatts.co.uk

*hardback